Mooseltoe
A Moose and A Dream

Once upon a wintry day
in a land covered white like foam.
Located near the cold North Pole
and the site of Santa's home.
A dwelling stands here much like yours
full of laughter, full of song,
the Christmas tree's lit, the stockings all hung
and yet there's something wrong.

The Moose clan is residing here
they are stunned beyond belief.
It's thier Son, named Mooseltoe
who is causing all this grief.

"I want to be a flying deer",
shouted Mooseltoe on this day,
"to rise and soar through frosty air
singing Jingle Bells all the way."

"There's absolutely nothing else
that I would rather try
than hitch myself to Santa's team
and with the reindeer...fly!"

His sister laughed hysterically
his dad was so appalled
this was the most ridiculous thing
that anyone recalled.

Late that night while Mooseltoe
tossed and turned in bed
his mom sat down right by his side
and this is what she said:
"If there's no way to keep you from
this foolish crazy thing,
it's time you leave your family
and find the great MOOSEKING

They kissed and hugged; he fell asleep,
as night turned into day.
He packed his bag, he said goodbye
and he was on his way.

Ignoring them he flapped his paws
he'd run and then he'd jump
but every time he tried to fly
Sppplatt! Right on his rump.

While sitting there he thought and thought
how he might leave the ground
what's that? A desperate cry for help?
A very scary sound.

He saw a walrus flailing
who'd fallen in a lake
"Grab my antlers," yelled Mooseltoe
"Hold on for goodness sake!!"

Back and forth and in and out
they struggled and they tried
Finally with one mighty pull
the walrus landed by his side.

"I was out there fishing all alone,
I heard a thunderous crack.
The ice beneath me broke in half.
With no way to get back."

"I have no friends," he sadly said
and continued where he sat.
"They laugh and say such nasty things,
just because I'm fat."

"If anyone can sympathize,
I'm the one who could."
He told the walrus his own tale
and the walrus understood.

They joked and laughed and shared their dreams.
They talked all through the night.
The two of them became great friends
and promised they would write.

They hugged and wished each other well.
The Moose, back to his quest.
But a blinding blizzard forced the Moose
to find a cave and rest.

He tossed and turned while dreaming
then a vision formed so clear.
A booming voice said "I'm MOOSEKING...
What are YOU doing here?"

"I w-w-w-want to fly with S-S-S-Santa Claus"
   A nervous Moose told the King
"I've tried so hard! I want to fly
   more than anything!"

"You must believe," echoed the voice
" the secret lies in you.
   You must believe and trust yourself,
   to make your dreams come true."

You must reach down, down deep inside
   and trust that you'll succeed.
   Just look inside your own Moose heart
   and find all that you need."

"I DO believe!" Said Mooseltoe
   the King called, "Keep on trying.
   Just hold that picture in your head"
"I see myself!! I'm flying!"

As quickly as he'd gone to sleep
he woke with such a start.
The answer lay inside of him
right there in his heart.

The Moose ran outside the cave
into a polar bear
who Santa sent to find the Moose,
he'd been looking everywhere.

Panic gripped the cold North Pole.
The time was getting late.
Pack the sleigh? un-pack the sleigh?
Would Christmas have to wait?

The elves all shouted "What is that?
Up there!! Look in the sky!
A miracle! Can this be true?
That moose has learned to fly?"

Mooseltoe landed in the square
to cheers and shouts...Hooray!
Santa hugged and thanked the Moose
for saving Christmas day.

And so the tale of Mooseltoe
lives on in fabled glory
we tell it here so you will know
the meaning of this story.

You needn't be like all the rest.
Trust and you'll achieve.
The secret lies within your heart
Just let yourself believe.

Special Thanks...

George Kramer
Terry Kippenberger
Paul Allan
Ray Disco
mckenna Jane Frentz

To order additional books, or for information
regarding the "Live" Stage production
of MOOSELTOE the "Moosical"
please visit
mooseltoe.com

CPSIA information can be obtained
at www.ICGtesting.com
Printed in the USA
BVHW021816191118
533544BV00010B/124/P

* 9 7 8 1 4 9 3 6 1 6 0 5 3 *